PUSHKIN PRESS CLASSICS

THE HUNTING GUN

'A humane and searching world view'
SPECTATOR

'Yasushi Inoue writes hand-in-hand
with Death, with a finger on the trigger'
LIRE

'Inoue wrote compassionately, but
without a hint of sentimentality'
TLS

T0190679

YASUSHI INOUE (1907–1991) worked as a journalist and literary editor for many years, beginning his prolific career as an author in 1949 with the novel *Bullfight*. He went on to publish fifty novels and 150 short stories, both historical and contemporary, becoming one of Japan's major literary figures. In 1976 Inoue was presented with the Order of Culture, the highest honour granted for artistic merit in Japan.

MICHAEL EMMERICH (b. 1975) is a translator, editor and assistant professor at the University of California, Santa Barbara. His many translations include works by Yasunari Kawabata, Genichiro Takahashi and Banana Yoshimoto.

THE
HUNTING
GUN

YASUSHI
INOUE

TRANSLATED FROM THE JAPANESE
BY MICHAEL EMMERICH

PUSHKIN PRESS CLASSICS

Pushkin Press
Somerset House, Strand
London WC2R ILA

The Hunting Gun was originally published as 猟銃 (Ryōjū) in Japan.
This translation is based on the text in *Inoue Yasushi zenshū*
(*Collected Works of Yasushi Inoue*), Tokyo, Shinchōsha (1995–1997).

This translation first published by Pushkin Press in 2014
This edition published by Pushkin Press in 2024

1 3 5 7 9 8 6 4 2

ISBN 13: 978-1-80533-039-4

Designed and typeset by Tetragon, London
Printed and bound in the United Kingdom by Clays Ltd, Elcograf S.p.A.

www.pushkinpress.com

THE
HUNTING
GUN

I PUBLISHED A POEM titled "The Hunting Gun" in the most recent issue of *The Hunter's Friend*, a floppy little magazine put out by the Japan Hunters' Club.

Hearing this one might suppose that I am at least slightly interested in hunting, but in fact, having been raised by a mother with a violent dislike of all forms of killing, I have never so much as held an airgun in my hands. It just so happens that the editor of *The Hunter's Friend* is a high-school classmate of mine, and when he heard that even now, at my age, I haven't outgrown the habit of publishing my somewhat idiosyncratic poems in a privately printed journal some of my poet friends and I put out, he asked if I would contribute a piece to his magazine. Presumably he was only being polite, suggesting this on a whim as a way of making up for our having been out of touch for so long. That's all it was. Ordinarily I would have demurred without a moment's hesitation, seeing as the magazine focused so narrowly on a topic with which I had no connection, and because he had stipulated that the poem had to deal in some way with hunting; but as chance would have it I had recently been led to feel a certain poetic interest in hunting guns and their relationship to the solitude of the human condition, and I had just been thinking that I should write something on the topic one day. His magazine seemed like the best possible venue for such a work, so one night late in November, at that time of the year when the air finally starts growing painfully cold, I sat at my desk past midnight composing a sort of prose poem, after my own fashion, which I then mailed the next day to the editorial office of *The Hunter's Friend*.

Since this prose poem, "The Hunting Gun", has some slight bearing on what I am about to write, I might as well copy it out here.

Large pipe clamped between his lips, a setter just ahead, the man trudged up the path towards the summit of Mount Amagi, through early-winter brush, crushing hoar frost beneath his rubber boots. Twenty-five-cartridge belt, umber leather coat, a Churchill double-barrel shotgun resting on his shoulder—what is this creature that he must arm himself so forbiddingly with that life-destroying tool of white-gleaming steel? After we had passed each other on the path, I turned to look at the hunter's tall back, and for some reason my heart was deeply touched.

Ever since that day, from time to time, I find myself unexpectedly wishing, in a train station in the city, or late at night on a street lined with bars, that I could walk the way he had. Slow, silent, cold... When I see the hunter then, in my mind's eye, he is not on Mount Amagi, amidst that chilly early-winter landscape; instead, a desolate, dried-up riverbed extends itself, white, behind him. The brightly polished hunting gun leaves the imprint of its creeping weight on the middle-aged man, on his solitary spirit, on his body, all the while radiating an oddly bloody beauty of a sort you will never see when its sights are trained upon a living thing.

It was only when my friend sent me the issue in which the poem had appeared and I leafed through its pages that I realized how stupid I had been: true, the poem bore the somewhat too predictable title "The Hunting Gun", but it clearly had no place in the pages of a magazine like this; indeed, it stood in such clear opposition to all the references to "the hunter's way" and "sportsmanship" and "a healthful hobby" that the page given over to it seemed like a settlement, a special zone completely set off from its surroundings. Needless to say, this poem embodied my sense of the essential nature of the hunting gun, as I had poetically intuited it—at any rate, that had been my intention—and in this regard I saw no need to disparage what I had accomplished; if anything, I was proud. Everything would have been fine if the poem had been published in some different magazine, but this was the bulletin of the Japan Hunters' Club, a journal whose very mission was to promote hunting as the most salubrious of sports; in such a context, my view of the gun was bound to come across as, to some extent, heretical and unwelcome. Nothing could be done now, of course, but I felt for my friend, realizing how taken aback he must have been when he first held the manuscript in his hand—how reluctant, indeed, to publish it—and my heart ached when I considered the characteristic delicacy he had shown in going ahead and printing it anyway. I half expected that some member of the Hunters' Club might send me an indignant letter, but my anxieties were misplaced: not even a single postcard of that sort found its way into my mailbox. For better or worse, the nation's hunters had given my poem the cold shoulder. Or to be precise, in all likelihood they hadn't even read it. But one day, after perhaps two months had passed and the whole incident had faded from my mind, I received a letter from a man—a stranger to me—by the name of Misugi Jōsuke.

I remember reading some later historian's description of the calligraphy on an ancient stone tablet on Mount Tai as "recalling the brilliant whiteness of the sun after a storm has passed". It would be only a slight exaggeration to say that this was the impression I received from Misugi's writing on the large white envelope, fashioned from handmade Japanese paper, as I held it in my hand. That old tablet has long since been lost, and no rubbing has survived, so I have no grounds for imagining the particular grace and style its writing possessed; and yet as I regarded those large, highly accomplished cursive characters, written with such verve that the envelope barely seemed capable of containing them, I came gradually to perceive, beneath their obvious boldness and assertiveness, a sense of emptiness welling from within each character, and I found myself recollecting that historian's appraisal of the calligraphy on the tablet. I got the impression that, having generously steeped his brush in ink and taken up the envelope in his left hand, Misugi had dashed off the address in a single headlong rush, but I sensed in the lively strokes an odd coldness, a lack of expressiveness, a lack of engagement that had nothing to do with what is often described as a "settled" touch. I sensed in the freedom of the brush, that is to say, an utterly modern ego that refused to wallow blissfully in the act, unmarred by the subtle vulgarity and imperiousness of what is generally considered skilful calligraphy.

At any rate, the letter's dynamic, imposing air was enough to make it seem somewhat out of place when it turned up in my plain wooden mailbox. Cutting the seal, I found the same expansive, free-wheeling characters, five or six to a column, dashed out across the width of each extra-large sheet of *gasenshi*. "*I write to you as one with a fondness for hunting who not long ago had the opportunity to read your poem 'The Hunting Gun' in* The Hunter's Friend. *I am by nature an unsophisticated man with no affinity for the refinements of poetry; to be quite frank, this was the first time I had ever read a poem, and the first time, as well, I am sorry to say, that I had encountered your name. Reading 'The Hunting Gun', however, I was moved more deeply than by anything else in recent memory.*" That, more or less, was how the letter began. As I ran my eyes over these first lines, remembering the prose poem I had all but forgotten until then, it struck me that I had, at last, received the indignant protest I expected some hunter to send—and that it had been written, moreover, by a man of some standing. My heart tensed for a moment, but as I continued reading I realized that the letter's content was nothing like what I had anticipated. It came, indeed, as a complete surprise. His tone ever polite and respectful, yet at the same time tightly controlled, possessing the same coldly self-assured air as the handwriting, Misugi Jōsuke explained that he believed he himself was the man I had written about in "The Hunting Gun", and wondered if his suspicion was correct; that I must have glimpsed his lanky figure, his back, in the village at the foot of the mountain when he visited the hunting grounds on Mount Amagi early in November. His setter, specially trained for pheasant-hunting, white with black spots; the Churchill he had been given by his mentor when he lived in London; even his well-loved pipe had been favoured by my attention. He was honoured, if also somewhat embarrassed, that his distressingly unenlightened state of mind had touched a poetic chord in me, and could only marvel, belatedly, at the remarkable insight that characterizes that special breed of person, the poet. Having read this far, I tried

13

to call up the image he described, to paint in my mind's eye a fresh portrait of the hunter I had encountered on the narrow, cedar-lined path I had followed one morning five months earlier, in a village known for its hot springs at the foot of Mount Amagi, on the Izu peninsula; but apart from the vaguely solitary air that clung to the hunter's back, which was what had caught my eye in the first place, nothing came to me. I remembered a tall, middle-aged gentleman, but that was all: certainly not his appearance, or even the sense of his age that I might have gotten from his clothing.

Of course, I hadn't observed the man with special care. He had simply struck me, as he came along the path with his shotgun over his shoulder and a pipe in his mouth, as having a sort of pensiveness about him that one did not ordinarily see in hunters—an atmosphere that seemed, in the crisp early-winter morning air, so extraordinarily *clean* that after we had passed each other I couldn't help turning to look back. He had just stepped off the path onto a road that led through a dense wood up into the mountains, and as I watched him go, treading cautiously, one slow step at a time, taking care that his rubber boots did not slip on the surface of the road, which was fairly steep, something in his figure had suggested the profound loneliness I had described in "The Hunting Gun". Even I had recognized that his splendid hunting dog was a setter, but in my ignorance of hunting there was no way I could have identified the make of gun he was carrying. I only learnt much later, when I sat down to write my poem and did a little hasty research, that Richards and Churchills were the top hunting guns, and I had decided for my own reasons to furnish the gentleman I was writing about with an expensive English gun; it just happened that the shotgun the real Misugi Jōsuke owned was the same one I had chosen. Thus, having him come forward and introduce himself as the subject of my poem did very little for me: the living, breathing man behind the idea I had formed remained, even now, unknown.

Misugi Jōsuke's letter continued. *"You will no doubt be puzzled by what I am about to explain, coming as it does out of the blue, but I have here three letters that were addressed to me. I intended to burn them, but now, having read your poem and learnt of your existence, I find myself wanting to share them with you. I will send them, along with my sincere apologies for disturbing you, under separate cover; I hope only that should you have a moment to spare you might be so gracious as to peruse them, understanding that I have no other motive in sending them to you than this. I would like for you to understand the 'desolate, dried-up riverbed' you glimpsed within me. We humans are, in the end, stupid creatures who cannot help desiring that someone know us as we are. I have never felt such a yearning, but now that I know you are out there, and know of the special interest you have so kindly taken in me, I would like you to know everything. Once you have read the letters, you may destroy all three in my stead. I might add that when you saw me in Izu, it was most likely shortly after these letters came into my possession. My interest in hunting goes back several years, however, to a period when I was not as utterly alone as I am today, when my life, in both its public and its private dimensions, was without major disruption. Already, then, I could not do without the hunting gun on my shoulder. I mention this by way of closing."*

Two days after I read these words, the three letters arrived. Like the first, the envelope they came in bore the name "Misugi Jōsuke, Izu Inn". The letters had been written to him by three women, and when I read them... no, I will refrain from describing what I felt. I will simply transcribe the three letters below. I might note in conclusion, however, that although I checked various *Who's Who*s and social registers and the like, suspecting that this man Misugi must be a prominent member of society, his name did not appear in any of them, suggesting that it was a pseudonym he had adopted for the sake of his communications with me. Finally, I have filled in with the name he chose those of the numerous blacked-out spaces in the letters where the man's name had obviously once been legible, and I have altered the names of all the other people who appear within them.

Uncle, Uncle Jōsuke.

It's hard to believe three weeks have gone by since Mother died. People stopped coming to pay their respects yesterday, more or less, so all of a sudden the house has grown very quiet, and at last I can really feel how sad it is that Mother is gone. I'm sure you must be feeling totally worn out. I can't thank you enough for all you did, taking care of everything from planning the service to contacting all the relatives, even troubling yourself about food for the wake—and then on top of all that, since the circumstances of Mother's death were so unusual, going to talk so many times with the police for me. You truly thought of everything. And then of course you had to rush off immediately to Tokyo on business... I hope you don't get sick from having exerted yourself too much.

Assuming you were able to stick to the plan you had when you left, though, you should be done with everything in Tokyo by now, and be back in Izu gazing out at the beautiful woods—that bright but somehow cold and moody landscape I know so well, that looks like a picture on a china dish. I've put pen to paper, in fact, hoping that you will read this letter while you are still in Izu.

I was going to try and write the sort of letter that would make you want to go out and stand in the wind with your pipe in your mouth, but I don't have it in me. For some time now I haven't been able to get past this point—I don't know how many sheets of paper I've wasted. This isn't how I wanted it to be. I just wanted to explain very honestly how I'm feeling right now, so that you will understand, and I've planned out any number of times how to do it, I practised writing this letter, but the second I take up my pen everything I want to say washes over me all at once… no, that isn't really right, either. It's the sorrow that pours over me, like the white crests of the waves in Ashiya on a windy day, confusing me. I'll force myself to write, though, even so.

*

All right, Uncle—I'll still use this term of affection, as I always have—here goes: I know about what happened, about you and Mother. I learnt the whole thing the day before she died. Because I read her diary without her knowing.

I can't even imagine how awful it would have been if I'd really had to say those words. I probably couldn't have got a single word out, no matter how hard I tried to stay calm. I was only able to do it because this is a letter. Not because I'm shocked, or scared. I just feel sad. So sad my tongue goes numb. Not sad about you, or about Mother, or myself. It's everything, all around me—the blue sky, the October sunlight, the bark of the crape myrtle, bamboo leaves rustling in the wind, and the water and the stones and the earth, all of nature, all I see, takes on this sad colouring the second I open my mouth to speak. Ever since I read Mother's diary, I've started noticing that maybe two or three times a day, or sometimes even five or six, the whole natural world, everything around me, is suddenly awash with a sad colour, as if the sun is setting. All I have to do is remember you and Mother and my world is completely transformed. Did you know, Uncle, that in addition to the thirty or so colours such as red and blue that you find in a paintbox, there is a separate sad colour, and that this sad colour is something you can really see?

What happened between you and Mother has shown me that there is such a thing as love no one blesses, love that must not be blessed. Only the two of you, no one else, could ever know how much in love you were. Not Aunt Midori, not me, not any of our relatives. None of our neighbours, not the people across the street, not even your best friends knew—and they couldn't. Now that Mother has died, only you know. And when you die, Uncle, not one person on this planet will even suspect that this love of yours existed. Until now, I always believed love was as bright as the sun, dazzlingly so, and that it should be eternally blessed by God and all the people around you. I knew love was like a clear stream that sparkled beautifully in the sun, and when the wind blew any number of soft ripples skittered across its surface, and its banks were gently held by the plants and trees and flowers, and it kept singing its pure music, always, as it grew wider and wider—that's what love was to me. How could I have imagined a love that stretched out secretly, like an underground channel deep under the earth, flowing from who knew where to who knew where without ever feeling the sun's rays?

For thirteen years Mother deceived me. She was still deceiving me when she died. I never dreamt we could have any secrets from each other, no matter what happened. She used to say so herself, that we were mother and daughter, after all. The only thing she never talked about was the reason she and Father had to break up; she said I wouldn't understand until it was time for me to get married myself. That made me want to grow up as quickly as I could. Not because I wanted to know what happened between Mother and Father, but because I thought having to keep that knowledge bottled up inside her must hurt Mother a lot. And it did, in fact, seem to be very painful. It never even occurred to me, though, that Mother might be keeping an altogether different secret from me!

When I was a girl, Mother used to tell me this story about a wolf who was enchanted by the devil and tricked a little rabbit. The wolf was turned into a stone for what he did. Mother tricked me, and she tricked Aunt Midori, and she tricked everyone else… it's just incomprehensible. The devil who enchanted her must have been one terrible devil. Come to think of it, Mother used the word *wicked* in her diary. The two of you were going to be *wicked*, she said, and if you were going to do it anyway you might as well be thoroughly evil. Why didn't she write that she had been possessed by the devil? My poor mother, so much unluckier than the wolf who tricked the rabbit! And to think someone as gentle as Mother, and as gentle as you, Uncle Jōsuke, whom I love so much, could have decided to be wicked—to be evil, in fact! How heartbreaking to love someone, but only be able to hold on to that love if you give yourself up to evil! When I was a girl, someone once bought me a round glass paperweight with a fake red petal inside it during the festival for Shōten at the temple in Nishinomiya. I took it in my hand and started walking, but before long I began to cry. I'm sure at the time no one understood why I had suddenly burst into tears. I had been overcome by sadness, all at once, because I imagined how that petal must feel, frozen in the cold glass, motionless, even when spring came, and then when autumn came, poor petal, crucified in the glass. I feel the same sadness now. Your poor love, sad as that petal!

*

Uncle, Uncle Jōsuke.

You must be very angry with me for secretly reading Mother's diary. But the day before she died, I had a premonition, I guess you could say—a feeling that came over me all at once, just like that, that she wasn't going to recover. Her death was getting closer. I felt it in her somewhere, something bad. You know as well as I do, Uncle, that for the past six months there seemed to be nothing wrong with her except for a slight, persistent fever—she still had her appetite, and in fact her cheeks glowed more than before, and she put on weight. But recently when I saw her from behind, when I looked at the line from her shoulders down to her arms, especially, she seemed so forlorn that I felt a kind of foreboding. The day before Mother died, Aunt Midori came by for a visit, and when I went to

Mother's room to tell her and slid her door open I was so surprised that I almost gasped. She was kneeling on the floor facing the other way, wearing a *haori* of greyish-blue Yūki silk with a large thistle woven across the back. She had told me once that I could have it because it was too gaudy for her at her age, and then she had wrapped it in paper and put it away in the chest of drawers, and for years she had almost never taken it out. I couldn't stop myself from crying out.

"Is something wrong?" Mother turned to face me, looking puzzled.

"I mean… " I started, but then I couldn't continue. A second later I couldn't even see why I had been so taken aback in the first place, and the whole thing seemed funny. Mother loved kimono, and she used to take out old, flashy pieces and try them on all the time—in fact, when she got sick it became almost part of her daily routine to take some kimono she hadn't worn in years out of the chest and put it on, and she had been choosing bolder and bolder designs, maybe to cheer herself up. When I thought about it later, though, I realized that it really had been a shock to see her in that Yūki *haori*. Because she was so beautiful it was like being woken up all at once from a deep sleep—I'm not exaggerating. And at the same time, I had never in my life seen her looking as lonely as she did at that moment. Aunt Midori was behind me, and when she stepped into the room she commented right away on how lovely Mother looked, and then sat for a time without speaking, lost in admiration.

The beautiful but lonely feeling that came over me when I saw Mother in that *haori*, sitting with her back to me, stayed there inside me all day, like a cold weight that had settled in my heart.

In the evening, the wind that had been blowing since morning died down, so Sadayo and I raked up the leaves that had fallen in the garden and burned them. While I was at it, I thought I would bring out a bundle of straw I had bought a few days earlier for way too much and burn it to make ash for Mother's *hibachi*. As I was doing that, Mother, who had been sitting inside, watching me through the glass doors, came out onto the verandah with a package wrapped in clean brown paper.

"Burn this too, please!" she said.

When I asked what it was, she snapped in an unusually sharp tone that it was nothing, just burn it. I guess she felt bad, though, because she said softly, "It's a diary. My diary." She told me once more that she wanted it burnt, and then she spun on her heel and walked off down the hall, her gait oddly unstable, as if she were being carried along by the wind.

It took about half an hour to make the ash. By the time the last straw had flared and gone up in a line of purplish smoke, I had made my decision. I took Mother's diary and quietly went upstairs to my room, and then hid it at the back of a shelf. That night, the wind blew up again. When I looked out of my window, the garden was bathed in the light of an almost ferociously white moon, and it had a sort of barren air, like some rocky coast up north, and the roar of the wind sounded like waves pounding the shore. Mother and Sadayo had gone to bed ages ago, so I was the only one up. I stacked five or six heavy encyclopedia volumes by the door so it wouldn't open right away if someone tried it, and I pulled the curtain all the way shut— even the moonlight pouring into my room scared me!—and then finally I adjusted the shade on my lamp and placed a single college notebook down on my desk. That notebook was what had emerged from the brown wrapping paper. That notebook was Mother's diary.

*

Uncle, Uncle Jōsuke.

I was scared that if I just let this opportunity go by, I would never learn what happened between Mother and Father. Until then, I hadn't wanted to know about Father, not until the time came for me to get married myself and Mother told me. I kept the name Kadota Reiichirō tucked away deep inside my heart, and that was enough. But when I saw Mother earlier that day, sitting with her back to me in the Yūki *haori*, I changed my mind. For some reason, I felt absolutely certain that Mother was not going to recover—I felt it in my heart.

At some point, I had learnt from my grandmother in Akashi and other relatives why Mother had to break up with Father. It had happened when I was five, and I was living in Akashi with

Mother, her parents and the maids while Father was at his university in Kyoto, doing research for his degree in the paediatrics department. One blustery day in April, a young woman came to see Mother with a newborn infant in her arms. As soon as she had come up into the house, she laid the baby down in the alcove, undid her *obi*, and started changing into an under-kimono she took from a little basket she had brought. Mother was stunned when she came back with the tea. The woman was genuinely crazy. Later, they learnt that the frail-looking baby in the alcove, dozing under the red nandina berries that had been hung there, was her child by my father.

Soon after that the baby died. Fortunately the woman's mental issues were just temporary, though, and she was back to her usual self almost immediately. I hear she married into a merchant household in Okayama, and she's still living there happily. Mother ran away from her parents' house in Akashi not long after that incident, taking me along, and Father, whom her parents had adopted so that he would be part of the family, ended up leaving it again. I remember my grandmother telling me when I started middle school, "There was no point making a stink, but then Saiko always was a stubborn one, even when there wasn't anything to be done." I guess the thought of forgiving him offended Mother's moral sense. That was as much as I knew about what had happened. Until I turned seven or eight, I thought Father was dead. They let me believe that. To tell the truth, even now, in my heart, Father is dead. I hear he runs a big hospital in Hyōgo, not an hour away, and that he has stayed single, even after all this time; but however hard I try I just can't imagine him, my real father. That man may be alive, in reality, but my father has been dead for ages.

*

I opened the first page of Mother's diary. And how surprised I was to find that the first word my hungry gaze landed upon was *sin*—yes, sin. Several times in a row—*SIN SIN SIN*—the handwriting so coarse I could hardly believe it was Mother's. And then, under all those piled-up *SIN*s, scrawled out as if the words themselves were being crushed by

31

their weight: "Oh Lord forgive me—Midori-san, forgive me." That was all I saw. The rest of the writing on the page had melted away, leaving just that one line, like a devil living there, glaring at me so fiercely it seemed it was about to spring.

I slammed the diary shut. I can hardly express how dreadful that moment was. The whole house was perfectly still, except for the loud pounding of my heart. I got up, checked that the door and the windows were still shut tight, and then I went back to my desk, screwed up my courage, and opened the diary again. I felt like the devil myself, now, as I read the whole thing—every word, from start to finish. But Mother hadn't written a single line relating to my father, the man I had been so curious about in the first place—the whole diary was focused on her relationship with you, things I never even dreamt were possible, spelt out in language so wild I would never have imagined Mother had it in her. Sometimes she suffered, sometimes she was overjoyed, sometimes she prayed, or despaired, or resolved to die—yes, it's true, she made up her mind any number of times to commit suicide. She would kill herself if Aunt Midori ever learnt about her relationship with you, that was her plan. She always seemed so bright, to enjoy talking with Aunt Midori... who could have guessed she was so terrified of her?

Reading her diary, I learnt that for thirteen years Mother lived with the weight of death always bearing down on her shoulders. Sometimes the entries would continue four or five days in a row, and then for two or three months she wouldn't write a word, but it was clear on every page that Mother was face-to-face with death. *"Yes, why don't you just die, if I were dead all my problems would be solved..."* Oh, what could have made her write such desperate, unthinking words? *"What need have I to be afraid of anything, now that I have resolved to die? Forget your shame, Saiko! Be more bold!"* What could have led a woman as gentle as Mother to write something so careless and self-centred? Was it really love? That beautiful, shining thing we call love? You gave me a book for my birthday one year, Uncle, with a picture of a naked woman standing tall and proud by a beautiful fountain, her long, full hair streaming around her chest, cupping her hands around her slightly upturned, bud-like breasts... This, the book explained, was love. But oh, Uncle, the love you and Mother shared was nothing at all like that!

Now that I have read Mother's diary, Aunt Midori scares me more than anything else in the world, just as she did Mother. I've inherited the pain of Mother's secret. Aunt Midori, who used to pucker up her lips and kiss my cheek! Aunt Midori, whom I loved every bit as much as Mother! I'm pretty sure that when I started first grade in Ashiya, Aunt Midori was the one who gave me a new backpack with giant roses all over it. And when I went on my first school trip to the seaside in Tangoyura, she gave me a big inflatable ring that looked like a seagull. For the arts festival in second grade, I told the story of Tom Thumb—the Grimm brothers fairy tale—and when I got all that applause, it was because Aunt Midori had kept listening to me practise, night after night, giving me rewards when I did a good job. And I could keep going and going—Aunt Midori is there in all my childhood memories. Mother's cousin, her closest friend. Now Aunt Midori only dances, but she used to be so good at mahjong and golf and swimming and skiing. The pies she baked were bigger than my face. I remember she came over once with a whole group of Takarazuka actresses to surprise us. Oh, why has Aunt Midori always been such an important part of our lives, filling it with her bright light, as carefree as a rose?

*

I don't know if people really have premonitions, but I had something like that about you and Mother once—just once. It was about a year ago. I was going to school with my friends, and when we got to Hankyū Shukugawa Station, I realized I had left my extra-curricular English reader at home. So I asked my friends to wait for me and went back alone to get it, and then when I came to our gate, for some reason I just couldn't go in. The maid had been out running errands all morning, so I knew Mother was the only one in the house. And yet somehow, her being there all alone made me uneasy. I was scared. I stood outside the gate for a while, staring at the azaleas, trying to decide if I should go in or not. In the end I gave up on my reader and walked back to Shukugawa, where my friends were waiting.

It was really weird—even I couldn't say why I had acted that way. I had the feeling that from the moment I walked out of the gate to go to school, just a little while before, a time that belonged only to Mother had started flowing through the house. And she wouldn't want me to intrude, she would look very sad if I did—that was the sense I had. So I went back along the street beside the Ashiya River, feeling an indescribable loneliness, kicking stones as I went, and when I got to the station I sat in the waiting room, leaning against the bench, hardly hearing my friends talking.

Nothing like that had happened before, or ever happened again. It fills me with horror, though, just thinking that I could have such a premonition. How frightening are the things we have inside us! Who knows, maybe at some point, somewhere along the way, Aunt Midori had exactly the same sort of baseless intuition that I had? How can we be sure that she didn't? When we played cards, she was always so proud that she could sniff out what her opponents were thinking—her nose was even better than a pointer's. Oh, just the thought makes my blood run cold. Of course, I know it's silly of me to worry, that she probably never knew. And it's all over now. The secret has been kept. No, it wasn't just kept—Mother died to protect it. I'm sure of that.

On that awful day, just before Mother began suffering so terribly—her pain was so excruciating that I couldn't even watch, even though it lasted only a little while—Mother called me to her side. Her skin was so eerily smooth then that she looked like a puppet. "I took poison just now," she said. "I'm tired, too tired to go on living." Her voice was so strangely clear that it was like listening to music from heaven, as if she weren't speaking to me at all, but through me to God. And then I heard, very distinctly, the sound of that stack of words I had seen in her diary the night before—*SIN SIN SIN*, piled as high as the Eiffel Tower—crashing down on top of her. The whole weight of the building she had erected from her sins over the course of the past thirteen years, all those floors, was crushing her exhausted body, carrying it off. And then, as I sat on the floor by her futon, weary and dazed, following her distant, unfocused gaze with my own, I felt a sudden surge of anger, like

37

a tempest blowing up from a valley. Something like anger, anyway. An indescribable resentment towards something, seething and boiling away inside me. I kept looking at Mother's sad face, and I said nonchalantly, as though none of what was happening had anything to do with me, "Oh? Did you?" And the next second, my heart felt cold and clear, as if someone had poured water over it. I got up, so calm and collected that even I felt kind of surprised at myself, and then, without taking a short cut across the room to go out the other side, I went into the hall and turned the corner, feeling like the floor was made of water—this was when I heard Mother start screaming from the pain as death's muddy torrent surged over her—and I went down the long hall into the little room at the end where we kept the telephone, and called you, Uncle. Five minutes later someone threw the front door open on its track with a great clatter and stumbled up into the house, but it wasn't you, it was Aunt Midori. And so, when Mother breathed her last, Aunt Midori, whom she had been closer to than anyone, and whom she had feared above all else, was holding her hand, and it was Aunt

38

Midori who spread a white cloth over Mother's face as she lay there, unable any more to feel pain or sadness.

*

Uncle, Uncle Jōsuke.

That first night, the night of the wake, the house was so quiet it was almost unearthly. The stream of visitors coming and going all day—the police, the doctor, the neighbours—had stopped just like that when night came, so only you and Aunt Midori and I were left kneeling in front of the coffin, and not one of us said a word, as if we were all concentrating on the soft lapping of water somewhere outside. Each time an incense stick burned out, we took turns rising to light another and pray before Mother's photograph, or gently open a window to clear the air. You seemed saddest of us all, Uncle. Whenever you got up to light a new stick, you would peer intently at Mother's picture, unmoving, a look in your eyes that was calmer than anything, and then, still wearing the same sorrowful look, you would smile ever so faintly—so faintly that no one else would even see it. I can't tell you how many times I found myself thinking, that night, that however much Mother suffered, maybe in the end one has to say that she lived a happy life.

Around nine o'clock, when I had stood and gone over to the window, I suddenly burst out crying. You came and rested your hand gently on my shoulder, and stayed for a moment without speaking, and then you went silently back and sat down. What made me cry, then, wasn't a sudden welling-up of sadness at Mother's death. I had been remembering how, earlier in the day, when Mother spoke for the last time, she hadn't mentioned you or even said your name, and then I'd started wondering why, when I called and told you what had happened, you hadn't come rushing over yourself, you, not Aunt Midori, and as I thought about it all a deep sadness suddenly took hold of me. It struck me that your love for each other, the love that had made it necessary for you to keep play-acting until the last, was as unfortunate as that petal crucified in the glass. Then I got to my feet and opened the window, and as I was standing there looking up at the cold, starry sky, struggling to keep my sadness from overflowing,

I had the thought that at that moment Mother's love was climbing up into the blackness, unknown to anyone, unseen, speeding up through the stars, and then I just couldn't bear it any more. My own sadness at the death of the woman I had known as my mother couldn't compare, I thought, to the profundity of the sadness of that love that was rising into the sky right then.

At dinner, as we were about to start eating our sushi, I burst into tears again.

"You must be strong," Aunt Midori murmured quietly, gently. "It hurts me so that I can't do anything to help."

When I wiped away my tears and glanced up, Aunt Midori was watching me, her eyes brimming just like mine. I gazed into those beautiful, moist eyes and shook my head without saying anything. I doubt she paid any attention to that gesture. But the truth is, I had started crying because suddenly I pitied her. Aunt Midori arranged some sushi on a plate as an offering to Mother, then took some for you, and for me, and then finally for herself, and as I watched her transfer the pieces of sushi onto each of the four plates, for some reason I felt that she was the most unlucky of us all, and that feeling came out of me in the form of sobbing.

I cried once more that night. This was after you and Aunt Midori told me I should get some sleep so I would be ready for everything the next day, and I spread my futon in the other room and lay down. I was so worn out from dealing with people all day that I fell asleep immediately, but then I started awake, drenched in sweat. I looked at the clock on the staggered shelves in the alcove and saw that about an hour had passed. The next room, where the coffin was, was still just as quiet as before; apart from the occasional click of your lighter, I didn't hear a sound. Then, after thirty minutes or so, you and Aunt Midori had a brief exchange.

"Why don't you rest a little," you said. "I'll stay up."

"I'm all right. Why don't you go."

That was all. After that, it was silent again; no matter how long I waited, nothing broke the stillness. I sobbed violently for the third time as I lay on my futon. You and Aunt Midori probably didn't hear me that time. I cried then because the whole world seemed so lonesome and sad and scary. You and Mother, who was a Buddha now, and Aunt Midori—the three of you were all there together, in the same room. Each of you was silent, lost in your own thoughts. The adult world was so lonesome, scary and sad that I could hardly bear it.

*

Uncle, Uncle Jōsuke.

I know I've been rambling. But I wanted to explain to you exactly how I feel right now, so that you will understand the favour I am going to ask of you.

This is what I want: never to see either you or Aunt Midori again. I can't take advantage of your kindness the way I used to, in all my innocence, before I read that diary, and I can't continue to be as trustingly selfish as I've always been with Aunt Midori. I want to get away from here, from the rubble of words that crushed Mother, all that sin. I don't have the energy to say anything more.

I plan to leave this house in Ashiya in the care of a relative in Akashi, a man named Tsumura, and then, at least for the time being, go back to Akashi

43

and open a small dress-making shop so that I can support myself. In the letter Mother left for me when she died, she said I should go to you whenever I needed help or advice, but if she had known me as I am now I know she would not have said that.

I burned Mother's diary in the garden today. That single college notebook was reduced to almost nothing, just a handful of ash, and while I was off fetching a bucket to douse it a little whirlwind blew up and carried the ash away somewhere with the fallen leaves.

I will send a letter Mother wrote to you under separate cover. I found it when I was going through the things in her desk the day after you left for Tokyo.

Mr Misugi Jōsuke,

Writing the characters of your name in this proper manner, I find, despite my age—not that thirty-three is all that old—that my heart begins to flutter, as if this were a love letter. Looking back over the past decade, I am puzzled to realize that, while I have written dozens of love letters, some in secret but others quite openly, not one was ever addressed to you. One finds it difficult to comprehend. I do not mean this as a joke; I have been mulling earnestly over this, and it has left me feeling an odd, rankling sort of incomprehension. Does it amuse you, perhaps, that I should feel this way?

Some time ago, Mr Takagi's wife—you remember her, I am sure... the woman whose face makes her look like a fox when she gets all dressed up—offered her appraisal of various notable personages of the Hanshin region, and when she arrived at you she made several very impolite pronouncements: that you were not a man to make a woman happy; that you hadn't a clue about the delicate workings of the feminine heart; that you might fall for a woman, but no woman could possibly fall for you. It goes without saying that Mrs Takagi uttered these unfortunate words under the influence of some degree of inebriation, and you need not take her evaluation so very seriously; still, you know as well as I do that there is that side to your character. You live, I think it is fair to say, a life entirely free of loneliness. You are not one to yearn for companionship the moment you are on your own. You may sometimes look bored, but never lonesome. And you have a tendency to see things in an oddly clear-cut fashion, and to be absolutely convinced of the superiority of your own views. You may say this is merely a sign of confidence, but watching you one is possessed somehow by an urge to seize you and give you a shake. In a word, I suppose one might describe you as a man utterly intolerable to women, completely devoid of an endearingly human side, who in no way makes it worth the trouble of doing you the favour of falling for you.

Perhaps, then, I am demanding too much of you in my fretful attempts to communicate some sense of

my befuddlement at the absence, among the dozens
of love letters I have penned, of even one bearing
your name. Nevertheless the feeling remains. Surely
I could have written you one or two, at least? To be
sure, from a certain perspective one might argue
that, while the epistles were not addressed to you,
the emotions I felt during their writing *were*—they
simply ended up in the wrong hands, and thus, as
far as my sentiments were concerned, I might as
well have been addressing you. My retiring nature
inhibited me, a grown woman, from plying my
husband with cloyingly intimate letters of the sort
one might expect of a young and inexperienced
girl, that was the difficulty—and so I dashed off
letters to other men, men towards whom I felt no
such diffidence. I suppose in the end the stars simply
were not aligned in my favour, so to speak—I was
born to this misfortune. And it was yours, as well.

> What are you doing now
> I wonder, knowing full well
> that if I were to approach
> your lofty repose might
> crumble

This is a poem I composed last autumn as an outlet for my mood on a day when you were holed up in your study and my thoughts kept turning to you. You were staring at a Yi-dynasty porcelain or some such thing, waiting to see which of you would blink first, and I was unwilling to disturb your peace—or rather, I knew of no means by which I could possibly disturb it, much as I may have liked to… Oh, my dear husband, how maddeningly well you hold your fortress, impenetrable on every front!… and this work brims with your poor wife's sorrow at that moment. You will say I am a liar, no doubt. But even if I do stay up all night playing mahjong, there is still time enough for me to turn my feelings, like surreptitious glances, towards the annexe and your study. Needless to say, even this poem did not find its way to you: in the end, I left it in Dr Tagami's apartment, laying it softly on his desk—Dr Tagami, the young philosophy buff who, I suppose, is no longer simply a young philosophy buff, having been happily promoted this spring from his post as a lecturer to become a fully fledged assistant professor—with the result, as you are aware, that the young scholar's lofty, spiritual repose does indeed seem to have been pointlessly ruined.

My name turned up in tabloid gossip columns, causing you some degree of inconvenience. Earlier I noted the urge that comes upon me as I look at you to give you a vigorous shake; this little incident may, perhaps, have succeeded slightly in that direction; or it may not.

*

Carping on about such things will, however, only heighten your displeasure. Better to move on to the main argument.

I wonder what you think of all this. Looking back, it occurs to me that quite a long time has passed since we became husband and wife in name only. Does it not strike you that it would be a profound relief to put an end to our relationship? True, it is sad that it has come to this, but in the absence of any substantial objections on your part, I cannot help feeling that it would be best to devise some means of setting both of us, you as well as me, at liberty. How does this sound?

Now that you will be resigning from active participation in all your business activities—it came as a deep shock, I might add, to learn that your name was on the list of purged businessmen—it seems like the ideal moment, from your perspective, as well, to end this unnatural relationship. Here, briefly, is what I desire: our homes in Takarazuka and Yase. Those two will be sufficient. Lately I have been mulling, presumptuously enough, over the various possibilities open to me, and I have arrived at the conclusion that I would like to live in Yase, as the house there is of a fitting size and the environment is congenial to me, and to support myself for the remainder of my life with funds raised by selling the house in Takarazuka, for which I would ask two million yen or thereabouts. Think of this as one final illustration of my selfishness, and simultaneously as the first and only time I have ever allowed myself, or ever will allow myself, to lean upon you, asking for evidence of your affection.

The fact that I am making this unexpected proposal should not be taken to indicate that I have at present anything as stylish as a lover, let alone more than one. There is, therefore, no need for you to fret over the possibility that someone might relieve me of the money. Indeed, I regret to say that I have never yet found a potential lover who would not shame me. Seldom does one encounter a man who satisfies even my two most basic requirements: that he tend properly to the hairline on the nape of his neck, keeping it fresh as the cut edge of a lemon; and that the line of his waist be as clean and strong as a serow's. Sadly, the joy your bride took in her beloved husband a decade ago, when you first made her heart yours, remains to this day sufficiently overpowering. And speaking of serow: I remember a story I once read in a newspaper about a young man found living naked with a flock of those wild goats out in the middle of the Syrian desert. How ravishing he was in that photograph! His cold profile, capped by a tangle of unkempt hair; the powerful allure of his lanky legs, capable, as the paper observed, of running at fifty miles an hour. To this day, the memory of that youth inspires a peculiar surging in my blood, unlike anything I have ever known with another man. It strikes me that the word "intellectual" was invented to describe that face; the word "wild" to describe that form.

In the eyes of one who has glimpsed such a youth, all other men seem equally common, drearily dull.

If at any point your wife ever felt even a few brief sparks of unchaste longing, that was the day—when she was drawn to the goat boy. Thinking of him now, picturing his taut skin moist with desert dew... but no, more than that it is the cool purity of his extraordinary fate that stirs up crazed waves in my heart even after all this time.

The year before last, I believe it was, there was a period when I became infatuated with a painter in the New Life School, a man by the name of Matsuyo. I would find it rather galling if you were to take as straight fact the rumours that circulated then. I recall that in those days there was a strangely sad gleam in your eyes, verging on pity, when you regarded me. Although I had done nothing to deserve your pity! Even so I was attracted to your eyes then, just a little. You were wonderful, even if you did not quite reach the goat boy's level. Why, when you had such a marvellous look in your eyes, did you not let them rove a little? Stoicism is not everything, you know. Your gaze remained fixed so steadily on my face that you might as well have been examining a piece of pottery. And so I myself became as crisp and cool as old Kutani ware; I was seized with the desire to go and rest somewhere, absolutely still, and so I went and sat for Matsuyo in his chilly studio. That said, I still greatly admire his architectural vision. He is perhaps somewhat too like Utrillo for his own good, it is true, but one would be hard pressed to find another painter currently active in Japan who is capable of suffusing into paintings of utterly hopeless buildings such a thoroughly modern aura of melancholy, and of doing so, moreover, with such understatement. As a person, though, he was no good. A total failure, in fact. If you stood as the marker for a hundred points, he would have been, at best, a sixty-five. He may have had talent, but there was something nasty about him; his features were well proportioned, but he was sadly lacking in grace. He looked comical rather than thoughtful with his pipe between his lips; he had the face of a second-rate artist whose works had absorbed everything good in him, and only what was good.

Then last year, in early summer, I believe it was, I showed some affection to Tsumura, the jockey who rode Blue Glory to victory in the Ministry of Agriculture and Forestry Cup. This time your eyes shone less with pity than with cold, contemptuous malice. At first I thought it was the leaves outside the windows that made them look so green when we passed in the hall, for example; later on I realized how ridiculously mistaken I had been. It was very sloppy of me, I admit. Had I recognized the true cause, I could have prepared myself mentally to cast back some answering gaze of my own, whether cool or warm! But in those days I was in the throes of a fascination with the beauty of speed that made my whole body go numb; your medieval approach to the demonstration of your feelings could not have been more alien to my sensibilities. I would have liked, at least once, to let you see the pure hunger to win that claimed Tsumura as he clung to the back of that peerless mare, Blue Glory, galloping in a beeline past more than a dozen other horses, one after the next. I know you, too, would have felt your blood rise on catching a momentary glimpse of his earnest, lovable form—I am talking, of course, about Tsumura, not about Blue Glory—through your binoculars.

When he was only twenty-two, that somewhat unruly-looking youth drove himself against the greatest odds to set two new records, all because he knew I was watching him through my binoculars. Never before had I witnessed such passion. So intent was he on earning my praise that he forgot me altogether once he was astride that dark-brown mare, transfiguring himself into a demon of speed. Yes, I lived then, above all, for the joy of seeing the love I felt up in the stands—it was, indeed, a species of love—be transformed into a passion as limpid as water that he then proceeded to stir, circling around and around that great 2,270-metre oval. I feel not a trace of regret for having given him as a reward three of my diamonds that had survived the war. But that young jockey was lovable only as long as he was perched on Blue Glory's back; the moment he descended to earth, he was just an imp incapable of appreciating even the flavour of a good cup of coffee. The dauntless, headlong drive to win that he had cultivated astride his horse made it somewhat more thrilling to take him around than that writer Senō or the one-time leftist Mitani, but he had nothing else to offer. This was why, in the end, I took the trouble to introduce him to a dancer I had taken under my wing—the eighteen-year-old with the slightly upturned lip—and even saw them through the wedding.

I fear my pleasure in chatting with you like this has led me from my topic. What I meant to say is that while I may withdraw to Yase, up there to the north of Kyoto, I am by no means prepared at this point to withdraw from the world. I have no intention whatsoever of going off and devoting myself to religious austerities. I will leave you to light your kilns and fire your tea bowls; I will grow flowers. I am told one can earn quite a lot sending flowers down to market at Shijō. With the old housekeeper and the maid and two young women I have my eye on we should be able to tend 100 or 200 carnations. For the time being, at least, men will be verboten; I have grown a trifle weary of your masculine rooms. I mean that. I am planning out my life in all earnestness, determined this time to make a fresh start, to find genuine happiness.

You may be surprised by my sudden request that we end our relationship—though, come to think of it, perhaps the opposite is true, and you have been perplexed all along by my failure to make such a request. I myself cannot help being profoundly touched, as I look back, by the fact that I managed to go on living with you for more than a decade. To some extent I have acquired a reputation as a wife of less than impeccable conduct, and I suspect you and I both have left others with the impression that we are an unusual couple; still, we have arrived at this juncture without suffering any social catastrophes, even serving pleasantly together, on occasion, as official go-betweens helping others towards marriage. In this respect, I hope you will agree that I fully merit your praise.

How extraordinarily difficult it is to write a goodbye letter. It is unpleasant to get all weepy, but it is also unpleasant to be overly brisk. I would like for us to make a clean break and to go our separate ways without hurting each other, but a peculiar sort of posturing seems to have found its way into my prose. Perhaps there is no helping it: a goodbye letter is what it is, and it will not be a thing of beauty, no matter who its author is. I suppose I might as well write in a cold and prickly style appropriate to the content. Forgive me, then, for returning your enduring coldness by writing the sort of unabashedly disagreeable letter that will make you turn still colder.

*

It was February 1934, the ninth year of the Shōwa era. I believe it must have been about nine o'clock in the morning when I saw you, dressed in grey Western clothing, walking along the cliff just below my second-floor room at the Atami Hotel. This happened so very, very long ago that it all seems lost in a dream-like haze. There is no need for you to agitate yourself; just listen. How my eyes smarted at the sight of the greyish-blue *haori*, an enormous thistle woven across its back, that the tall, beautiful woman who came stepping along behind you wore. I had not really expected my intuition to prove so utterly on the mark. In order to confirm it, I had subjected myself to the rocking of the night train, forgoing sleep entirely. To invoke an old conceit, I wished that I were dreaming, and that I would awake. I was twenty years old at the time—the same age as Shōko now. The shock, I must admit, was somewhat too rude for a newly-wed with no sense of what was what in life. I immediately summoned the bell-hop and, faced with his suspicions, invented some excuse and settled the bill; then, unable to remain a moment longer on that spot, I fled outdoors. I stood for a minute on the pavement outside the hotel, holding fast to the searing pain that smouldered in my breast as I briefly debated whether to descend to the shore or go to the station. I started along the road to the ocean, but before I had gone half a block I stopped. I stood staring out at a spot on the wintry ocean where the sunlight glittered against a Prussian blue so perfect it could have been squeezed from a paint tube and smeared across the water; then, changing my mind, I spun on my heel, turning my back on that scenery, and took the other road, the one to the station. Thinking back over the years, it seems that selfsame road has carried me all the way to this point where I stand today. Had I continued down the road to the ocean, towards the two of you, I do not doubt that I would be a different woman now. But for better or for worse, that was not the path I chose. It occurs to me that in all my life, that was the biggest fork.

Why didn't I continue down the road to the shore? For a simple reason. Because I could not banish my acute awareness that in no area could I possibly rival that gorgeous woman five or six years my senior, Saiko, whom I had always called "elder sister"—not in terms of the depth of my experience of life, or my knowledge, or my talents, or my looks, or my gentleness, or the grace with which I held my coffee cup, or in discussions of literature, or in my sensitivity to music, or in the application of my make-up. Oh, what humility! The modesty of a new wife of twenty, so pristine only the curving lines of a work of pure art could express it. I am sure you have had the experience of going for a swim in the ocean in early autumn and discovering that each little movement you make causes you to feel the water's chillness more intensely, and so you stand there without moving. That was precisely how I felt then: too frightened to move. Only much later did I arrive at the happy conclusion that it was only right that I deceive you the way you had deceived me.

Another time, you and Saiko were waiting in the second-class lounge at Sannomiya Station for an outward-bound express. This must have been a year or so after the Atami Hotel. I stood amidst a gaggle of girls on a field trip, bright as flowers, considering whether to enter the lounge. Yet another time, I stood outside Saiko's house staring up at the soft light filtering through the gap in a curtain on the second floor, the gate before me shut tight as a clam, trying to decide whether or not to ring the doorbell—ah yes, I can still see myself that night, standing for ages awash in the insects' shrill fiddling, as vividly as if the memory were imprinted on my eyelids. I have the sense that this was around the same time I spotted you at Sannomiya Station, but I cannot say whether it was spring or autumn. I have no feeling for the season when it comes to these memories. And there are many, many of them—things that would make you moan... Still, in the end, I did nothing. After all, had I not turned away from the road to the ocean that day at the Atami Hotel, even then? Yes, even then, even then... strangely, all it took was a vision of that achingly blue, glittering ocean, heaving itself up in my mind's eye, and the agony that had burnt my heart—that a second before had been barely under my control, threatening at any moment to explode into madness—would subside, as if it were a thin sheet of paper that I had peeled away.

Although for a while I came close to losing my mind, time appeared to resolve our problems, and our relationship became as smooth as it could conceivably have been. As you cooled, with the speed of a red-hot piece of iron plunged into water, I matched your coolness; and as I grew cold, you drew circles around me in your plummeting frigidity, until at last we found ourselves living here within this magnificently frozen world, in a household so cold one feels ice on one's eyelashes. I wrote *household*, but that isn't right—it has none of the tepidity or the human stench of a household. One might more accurately call it a fortress, as I am sure you will agree. For a decade now, we have been holed up in this fortress, you deceiving me, me deceiving you—though you deceived me first. Such distressing transactions we humans make! Our whole life together was erected upon the foundation of secrets each of us kept from the other. You reacted to my countless unforgivable trespasses sometimes with scorn, sometimes with disgust, at other times with

an expression that was sorrowful and yet indif-
ferent. Often I would holler from the bath for the
maid to bring me my cigarettes. I would extract
a movie programme from my handbag when I
returned home and wave it back and forth, fanning
the opening at the front of my kimono. I left trails
of Houbigant everywhere, in the rooms and the
hallways. I danced a little waltz after hanging up the
phone. I invited stars from the Takarazuka Revue to
come dine with me and had photographs taken of
us, me nestled in amongst them. I played mahjong
in a padded kimono. On my birthday, I asked that
even the maids wear ribbons and then threw a
raucous party to which only university students
were invited. Naturally I knew full well how deeply
all of this displeased you. But you never once repri-
manded me—you couldn't. And so there was never
any friction between us. Thus the fortress's calm was
preserved, nothing changing but the air, which grew
progressively drier and colder and more unpleasant,
like a desert wind. You went out with your hunting
gun to shoot at pheasants and turtle-doves; why,
then, were you incapable of firing a bullet into my
heart? You were deceiving me anyway, so why didn't

you go all the way—trick me more cruelly, trick me until I didn't even realize I was being tricked? A man's lies can sometimes elevate a woman, you know, to the very level of the divine.

*

I see now, however, that at some point there must be an end to this life I have endured for a decade, and to our bargaining. I know it because somewhere deep in my heart I have harboured this expectation, subtle but persistent: the hope that something will arrive, that even now it is wending its way in our direction! Only two possibilities present themselves as to the form this ending might assume. Either there will come a day when I stand quietly huddled against your chest with eyes closed, or I will plunge that penknife you brought me as a souvenir from Egypt with all my strength into your chest, sending up a spray of blood from the wound.

Which of these two endings, I wonder, do you think I prefer? In truth, even I am unsure.

That reminds me. This happened, I suppose, about five years ago—I wonder if you will remember. As I recall, you had just returned from your travels in the south. Having absented myself for two days, I returned home somewhat intoxicated, my gait uncertain, though it was not yet even evening. I had understood that you were in Tokyo on business, but for some reason there you were, back at home, sitting polishing your gun in the living room. "I'm back!" I cried, and then without another word I stepped out onto the verandah and sat down on the sofa with my back to you, feeling the play of the chill wind on my skin. The canopy for the outdoor dining table was propped against the eaves, and by some trick of the light it transformed part of the line of sliding glass doors enclosing the verandah into a mirror that reflected a portion of the room, and I could see you there rubbing the barrel of your gun with a white cloth. Worn out from too much play, feeling irritable and yet simultaneously too languid to lift a finger, I let my gaze linger on your figure as you went about your business, but without really focusing my attention. After wiping down the barrel, you replaced the breech-block, which you had also burnished until it shone; you raised the gun twice or thrice, resting

the butt against your shoulder; and then all of a
sudden you froze with the shotgun lifted and shut
one eye, as if you were taking aim. And I realized
that the barrel was pointing straight at my back.

Did you want to shoot me? I must confess it was
very interesting for me to try to discern whether,
at that moment, setting aside the fact that the gun
was not loaded, you possessed the desire to kill me.
I pretended I hadn't noticed a thing, closed my eyes.
Were you aiming at my shoulder, at the back of
my head, at my nape? I waited with bated breath,
expecting to hear at any moment the icy click of the
trigger breaking the stillness of the room. But the
click never came. If it had, I was ready—as eager
as if this were the first chance I had been granted
in many years to make my life worth living!—to
collapse in a dramatic, staged faint.

Unable to bear it any longer, I slowly opened my
eyes. You remained in the same posture as before,
your sights set on my back. I sat motionless for a
while, until all at once, for whatever reason, I was
struck by the absurdity of what we were doing,
and I shifted slightly, turned to look at the real you,
not the one in the mirror, upon which you swiftly

swung the point of your gun away, took aim at the rhododendron in the yard—the one we had transplanted from Amagi, which had bloomed for the first time that year—and then, at last, I heard you pull the trigger. Why didn't you shoot your faithless wife that day? I would venture to say that I had done enough then to deserve being shot. You wanted to kill me sufficiently badly, and yet in the end you would not pull the trigger! If you had fired, if you had refused to overlook my trespasses, if you had driven into my pulsing heart an unmistakable loathing for your person—then, perhaps, against all odds, I might have fallen meekly into your arms. Naturally, I might also have gone in the opposite direction, letting you have a taste of my own marksmanship. At any rate, you failed, and so, releasing my gaze from the rhododendron that had fallen in my stead, I tripped more shakily than necessary from the room, humming "Under the Roofs of Paris" or some such tune, and withdrew to my private sitting room.

*

Years passed after that without affording us any further opportunity to bring all this to its conclusion. This summer, the blossoms on the crape myrtle were more poisonously red than ever before. I felt a subtle quickening of anticipation, almost a hope, that something unusual might occur...

I visited Saiko for the last time the day before she died. I found myself confronted, then, quite out of the blue, after more than a decade, by what was unmistakably the same greyish-blue *haori* whose nightmarish image, in the glaring Atami sunlight that morning, had burnt itself onto my retina. The huge purple thistle hovering above the background, its outline sharp, seemed to weigh upon the frail shoulders of the woman, now somewhat emaciated, whom you loved. I commented, as I came into the room and knelt beside her, on how lovely she looked, struggling to calm myself; but then I began to wonder what she could possibly be thinking, wearing this *haori* in my presence, at this moment, and all at once my blood began to seethe, to course through my body, like boiling water. I felt powerless to restrain myself. Sooner or later, this woman's transgressions, the fact that she had stolen another woman's husband, and the humility of that twenty-year-old bride, would have to be dragged out into the courtyard before the magistrate. That moment, it seemed, had arrived. And so I reached down into my heart and brought out the secret I had kept so carefully hidden for more than a decade, and set it softly down before the thistle.

"It brings back memories, doesn't it?"

She gave a quick, almost inaudible gasp, and turned to face me. I met her eyes with a steady gaze. And I persisted; I did not look away. Because naturally it was she who should avert hers.

"You wore that when you and Misugi went to Atami together, didn't you? You'll have to forgive me. I'm afraid I was watching you that day."

As I had expected, the blood drained visibly from her face, the muscles around her lips twitched in the most ugly manner—I am not just saying this, I truly was struck by her ugliness—as she tried to find something to say, but in the end she could not pronounce a word; she simply lowered her face, and, yes, let her gaze fall, settling on her white hands where they lay crossed on her lap.

The thought bobbed into my consciousness, then, that *this* was the moment I had been living for all those years, and I felt a pleasure of the sort one might feel standing in a shower with the water washing down over one's skin. At the same time, in some other region of my heart, I sensed with an indescribable sadness that one of the two possible endings had at last settled into a shape, and was even now moving towards us. I lingered there, wallowing in that emotion, for quite a while. I was fine; I could have sat in that spot until I grew roots. How desperately she must have wanted to disappear, though, that woman! Eventually, for what reason I cannot say, she lifted her waxen face and stared fixedly at me, her eyes very still. I knew then that she would die. Death had sprung, just now, into her body. Otherwise she could never have looked upon me with a gaze so still. The garden clouded over for a moment, then was bright again. Someone had been playing the piano next door, but now, suddenly, the sound broke off.

"Don't let it worry you, I don't mind. You can have him!"

I got to my feet, went out to the verandah to retrieve the white roses I had left there when I came, put them in the vase on the bookshelf, adjusted the arrangement; and then, as I gazed down at Saiko where she sat slumped over again, at her wiry neck, it struck me—awful premonition!—that this would most likely be the last time I saw her.

"Please, there's really no need to fret. I've deceived you all these years, too. We're even."

Without even meaning to, I chuckled. And all the while, how perfectly she maintained her silence! From start to finish she simply sat there, speaking not a word, so still and quiet it almost seemed she had stopped breathing. The judgement had been handed down. Now she was free to do as she liked, as far as I was concerned.

With that, I strode swiftly out of the room, flicking the hem of my kimono up with movements so crisp and clean even I could feel it.

Midori! For the first time that day, I heard her cry out behind me. But I continued down the hall, around the corner.

"Are you all right, Aunt Midori? You're terribly pale."

I realized that the blood had drained from my face only when Shōko, who was coming along the hall with cups of black tea on a tray, drew my attention to the fact.

By now, I am sure, you see why it is impossible for me to remain with you any longer; or rather, why it is impossible for you to remain any longer with me. I have written at great length and said much that is distasteful; now, at last, it seems the final curtain can descend on ten years of painful bargaining. I have said more or less all I wanted to say to you. If possible, I would be grateful if you could reply, giving your consent to our divorce, before your stay in Izu is complete.

*

Come to think of it, I will close with one bit of unusual news. Today, for the first time in years, I went and cleaned your study in the annexe myself, rather than leave it to the maid. I was impressed by how settled it is—a very nice study indeed. The sofa is singularly comfortable, and the Ninsei pot on the bookshelf does much to enhance the atmosphere, like a blaze of flowers in the otherwise muted room. I wrote this letter in your study. The Gauguin does not quite suit the space, and if possible I would like to take it with me and hang it in the house in Yase; I took the liberty of removing it from the wall, hanging the snowy landscape by Vlaminck in its place. I also rotated the clothes in the drawer, setting out three winter suits, each paired with one of my particular favourites among your neckties. Whether or not you will be pleased, I cannot say.

SAIKO'S LETTER (POSTHUMOUS)

By the time you read this, my darling, I will no longer be among the living. I don't know what it's like to die, but I know all my joy, my pain, my suffering will be gone. All my feelings for you, this surge of emotion that keeps coming and coming whenever I think of Shōko, will have vanished from the face of the earth, just like that. There will be nothing left of me—not my body, not my heart.

And yet, hours or maybe days after I've died and entered that state, you will read this letter. And it will communicate to you all these feelings I hold within me now, while I live. It will tell you, just as if I myself were talking to you, things about me, my thoughts and feelings, that you never knew before. You'll listen to my voice as it comes through this letter as if I were still living, and you will be stunned, saddened, angry. You won't cry. But you will look at me with that terribly sad face of yours, which no one but me knows—I know Midori has never seen it—and tell me how silly I am. I can see your face clearly even now, and hear your voice.

All of which is to say that even after I die, my life will still be waiting here hidden in this letter until it is time for you to read it, and the second you cut the seal and lower your eyes to read its first words, my life will flare up again and burn with all its former vigour, and then for fifteen or twenty minutes, until you read the very last word, my life will flow as it did when I was alive into every limb, every little corner of your body, and fill your heart with various emotions. A posthumous letter is an astonishing thing, don't you think? I brim right now with the desire to give you something true in the fifteen or twenty minutes of life this letter holds—yes, at least that much. It scares me to be saying this to you at this late date, but it seems to me that while I was alive I never once let you see me as I truly am. Now, writing this, I am the real me. Or rather, this me, the one writing, is the only one that is real. Yes, this is real...

My eyes still remember how beautiful the foliage was on Mount Tennō, near Yamazaki, washed by the fine autumn rain. What made it so beautiful?

We stood under the eaves of the closed old gate of that famous tea house at Myōkian, just across from the station, waiting for the rain to end, gazing up at the mountain, which jutted up just behind the station, so huge and so close, and it was so beautiful it took our breath away. It was a sort of trick of the season, perhaps, that moment in November, and of the time of day, shortly before dusk. An effect of the particular atmosphere that day in late autumn, after an afternoon of intermittent drizzle—an array of colours so rich it was as if the whole mountain were dreaming them, colours so beautiful they made us afraid at the thought that we were going to climb up there, up the side of the mountain. Thirteen years have passed since then, yet the touching beauty of those leaves, on all the different trees, rises up before me as if I were there at this moment.

That was the first occasion you and I were ever able to spend time alone together. You had been dragging me to various spots on the outskirts of Kyoto since morning, and I couldn't have been more exhausted, mentally and spiritually. I'm sure you must have been worn out too. As we climbed the steep, narrow path up the mountain, you said all kinds of outrageous things. Love is a form of attachment. I'm attached to my tea bowls, and there's nothing wrong with that, is there? So how can it be wrong for me to be attached to you? And: We're the only ones, just you and me, who have seen this magnificent foliage, here on Mount Tennō. And we saw it with each other, together. There's no going back now. You sounded like a spoilt child, trying to wheedle your way into getting what you wanted.

All day long my heart had been straining, trying not to give in to you, and then suddenly it was as if you had pushed it down, and I relented—all on account of the silly, desperate things you said. The confused pity your reckless, overbearing statements evoked in me crystallized itself within my body— like flowers blooming everywhere inside me—as the joy of a woman in love.

It amazes me how easy, how simple it was to forgive my own infidelity when I had never succeeded in forgiving my husband, Kadota, for exactly the same failing.

*

Let us be wicked, you said. Wicked. You used that word for the first time when we stayed at the Atami Hotel. Do you remember? It was windy out, and the storm shutters on the window facing the ocean kept shaking and rattling all night. When you pushed it open around midnight to try and fix it, there was a fishing boat far out at sea that had caught fire and was burning high, bright red, like a cresset. People might be dying out there, we could see that, and yet the horror of it didn't touch us—we saw only how beautiful it was. The second you closed the shutter, though, I became uneasy. You opened it again almost right away, but by then the boat must have burnt up, because there wasn't a speck of light anywhere—just the dim, settled, bleary vastness of the ocean.

Until that night, I had still been struggling, deep in my heart, to break away from you. But after that night, after we saw the burning boat, an odd fatalism took hold of me. When you suggested we be wicked together, when you asked me to join with you and deceive Midori for the rest of our lives, I replied without a moment's hesitation that if we were going to be wicked anyway, we might as well be evil. We would trick Midori, yes, but not only her—everyone, the entire world. That night, for the first time since we began having our trysts, I was able to sleep peacefully.

I felt as if I had glimpsed, in that boat blazing on the water, unbeknownst to anyone, the fate of our hopeless love. Even as I write this, that scene, those flames bright enough to overcome the darkness, rise up before me. What I saw on the ocean that night was without doubt a figure, the perfect figure, of the distress, the fleeting, this-worldly writhing that is a woman's life.

*

There's no point losing ourselves in such reminiscences, though. These last thirteen years, which began in the moments I have been describing, gave us our share of pain and anguish, but I feel even so that I have been the happiest person in the world. Cradled as I always was by your great love, your caring, I may even have been *too* happy.

I looked over my diary earlier today. I couldn't help being struck by how often the words "death" and "sin" and "love" appeared there, and it made me feel—as if I didn't know well enough already—how difficult the long years we navigated together have been; and yet, when I held that notebook in my palm and felt its heaviness, it had a happy weight. I may have been tormented by an omnipresent awareness of sin, a constant refrain of *SIN SIN SIN*, and I lived every day of my life staring down a vision of death, telling myself that I would die if Midori ever found out, I would make my amends to her, when she finally learnt, by dying, but all this merely stands as a measure of how irreplaceable my happiness was.

*

But oh, oh, who would ever have suspected that, beside this happy person I have been speaking of—you'll find this a pretentious figure of speech, darling, but I don't know how else to express it—there was another, different me. It's the truth. Another woman lived inside me, of whose existence even I was unaware. Another me you didn't know, and could never have imagined.

I remember you told me once that each of us has a snake living inside him. You had gone to see Dr Takeda, in the science department at the university in Kyoto, and I passed the time while you were with him looking one by one at all the different snakes on display in a row of cases tucked away in a corner of a long hallway in that dismal brick building. By the time you came out of Dr Takeda's office half an hour or so later, the snakes were starting to get to me, and I felt a bit queasy. That was when you told me about the snakes—peering into one of the cases, you joked, "This is you, and this is Midori, and this is me… everybody has one of these inside him; there's nothing to be afraid of." Midori's snake was a small, sepia-coloured one from some southern region; the one you said was mine came from Australia, and while it was small, too, its body was covered all over in white speckles, and its head came to a point, sharp like a drill. I still don't know what you meant then. I never spoke with you about the snakes again, but somehow what you said stayed lodged in my chest, I remembered it, and every so often, when I was alone, I would wonder about what those snakes inside us were. Perhaps on some occasions they are egotism, and then jealousy, and then at other times destiny.

I haven't understood about the snakes, even now, but I know that you were right that day, because there really was a snake living inside me. It revealed itself to me for the first time today. I can't think of a better way to describe the other self I carried inside me, without knowing.

*

It happened this afternoon. Midori dropped by to look in on me, and when she arrived I was wearing that greyish-blue Yūki *haori* you had had sent up from Mito for me all those years ago—the one that used to be my favourite when I was younger. She seemed taken aback when she walked into the room and saw it, and for a second I thought she might comment on it, but she didn't, she just sat there without saying anything. I supposed even she was shocked at my admittedly inappropriate choice of clothing, and so, since I was in a somewhat mischievous mood, I intentionally kept silent.

Suddenly she shot me an oddly icy look. "Isn't that the *haori* you wore when you and Misugi went to Atami?" she said. "I was watching you that day, you know." Her face was terrifyingly ashen, and her tone was so sharp she might as well have been jabbing at me with a short sword.

At first I failed to grasp the implications of what she had said, but soon the enormity of it hit me. Without really thinking I straightened the front of the kimono and then, as if being more formal was the only appropriate response in this context, I sat up as tall as I could.

She's known everything, all these years!

I felt oddly calm, as if I were gazing at the ocean at dusk from far away, watching the tide come in. So you knew, you knew it all, I thought, feeling an urge, almost, to take her hand in mine and comfort her. The moment whose anticipation had cast me into such terror had at last come, it was happening right now, and yet when I looked around me there wasn't a trace of fear to be found. There was nothing between us but the quiet lapping of water, like waves on the seashore. The veil behind which we had hidden our secret for thirteen years had been brutally ripped away, but what I saw underneath it was not the death that had obsessed me so, but something I can hardly think how to describe, something like peace, quietness—yes, a peculiar feeling of release. I felt relaxed. It was as if some dark, oppressive weight had been lifted from my shoulders, and in its place I had been asked to carry nothing at all but an oddly moving emptiness. I felt that I had an enormous amount of thinking to do. Not about dark, sorrowful, frightening things, but about something vast and futile, and yet at the same time quiet and fulfilling. I was in a sort of drunken ecstasy, that's what it was—a feeling of liberation. I sat in a stupor, gazing into Midori's eyes, but seeing nothing. My ears heard nothing of what she was saying.

When I came to, she had just left the room and was scampering down the hall.

"Midori!" I called. Why, I wonder? I don't know. Maybe I wanted her to come sit with me some more, for ever. And maybe if she had come back, I would have said to her what I was really thinking, without any posturing: "Please let me be formally united with Misugi." Or perhaps I would have said the opposite, but with exactly the same feeling: "The time has come for me to return Misugi to you." I can't say which of those sentences would have come from my mouth. Midori kept going; she didn't come back.

I'll die if Midori ever learns! A comical daydream. And all that *SIN SIN SIN*—such vain prickings of conscience. I guess once you've sold your soul to the devil, you can only become a devil yourself. Perhaps these last thirteen years I have been deceiving God, deceiving even myself.

After that I sank into a deep, untroubled sleep. When I awoke Shōko was shaking me, and my joints ached until I could hardly move; it was as if thirteen years of weariness were finally taking their toll. I realized that my uncle from Akashi was sitting by my pillow. You met him once—he's a contractor, and he had stopped by to see me for just half an hour on his way to Osaka on business. He chatted aimlessly about this and that for a few minutes and then he had to leave. As he was tying his shoes in the entryway, though, he called out, "Kadota got married, by the way." Kadota... how many years had it been since I had heard that name? He was referring, of course, to my former husband, Kadota Reiichirō. As far as my uncle was concerned he was only sharing a bit of news, but I was stunned.

"When?" Even I could hear my voice shaking.

"Last month, or the month before. I hear he built a house in Hyōgo, next to the hospital."

"Oh?" It was all I could do to speak this one word.

After my uncle had left, I made my way slowly down the hall, one step at a time, until all of a sudden I swooned and fell sideways, clinging to one of the posts. Feeling my hands tighten themselves, all on their own, I stood staring out through the glass doors. It was windy, the trees were swaying, yet it was unsettlingly quiet; I felt like I was at an aquarium, peering through the glass at an underwater world.

"Oh, it's no good," I said, unsure myself what I meant.

Shōko was beside me by then. "What's no good?"

"I don't know, something."

Shōko giggled, and I felt her supporting me gently from behind. "Sometimes you say the oddest things! Come, you need to lie down."

With Shōko helping me I was able to walk more or less normally as far as my futon, but the second I sat down I felt everything around me crumble to the ground, just like that. I half knelt on the futon, my legs angled to the side, steadying myself with my hand. Overwhelmed as I was, I still struggled to contain myself while Shōko was there, but when she went off to the kitchen the tears began streaming down my cheeks like water wrung from a rag.

Until that moment, it would never have occurred to me that I'd be so stricken to hear that Kadota had married. I don't know why I reacted that way. After a time—I don't know how long it was—I spotted Shōko through the glass doors, burning fallen leaves in the garden. The sun had set by then, and the evening was quieter than any I had ever experienced in my life.

Ah, she's burning them already!

I murmured these words out loud, feeling somehow as if it had been decided all along that things would happen this way, and that I had known it, and then I got up and took my diary from its place at the back of my desk. Shōko was burning leaves in the garden today so she could burn my diary along with them. How could it be otherwise? I took my diary out onto the verandah, sat down on a wicker chair, and spent a little while leafing through it. That notebook, full of columns of "sin" and "death" and "love". The confessions of a wicked woman. The three words I had gone on carving into those pages for thirteen years had completely lost the sparkling vibrancy that had been in them yesterday; they were ready, now, to join the purplish smoke rising into the sky from the pile of leaves Shōko was burning.

I made up my mind to die after I'd given my diary to Shōko. In any event, I told myself, the time has come for me to die. Or maybe it would be more accurate to say, in this instance, not that I had made up my mind to die, but that I lacked the energy to live any longer.

Kadota had been single all those years, ever since our divorce. That was only because he had gone abroad to study and then been shipped off to the south during the war, so he had missed his chance to get married again, but none of that changed the fact that he had never taken another wife. I realize now that in some way I couldn't perceive, his remaining single had been a tremendous support to me, to the woman I am. You will have to believe me when I say that, while I had occasionally heard bits and pieces of news from relatives in Akashi, I never saw him again after we divorced, or wanted to. For years, his name never even entered my thoughts.

Night fell. When Shōko and the maid had retired to their rooms, I took one of the photo albums from my bookshelf. This album contained twenty-odd photographs of Kadota and me.

One day several years ago, Shōko had surprised me by saying, "Look, all the pictures of you and Father are pasted in so your faces overlap!" She hadn't meant anything by it, but it was true: purely by coincidence, those pictures, taken soon after we were married, had been pasted in on opposite pages, so that we would be face-to-face when the album was shut.

"Oh, you say such ridiculous things!"

We said no more about it, but Shōko's words stuck in my heart, and once a year or so, at the oddest moments, they would pop into my mind. I had left the photographs as they were, though, until now—I never removed them, or replaced them

90

with others. But today I felt that it was time for me to take them out. So I lifted all the photographs of Kadota from the pages and slipped them into Shōko's red album, so that she would have them to keep, as pictures of her father when he was young.

*

This was the other me, then, whose existence even I knew nothing about. In this fashion, this very morning, the Australian snake you once said I had hiding inside me, covered with little white speckles, revealed itself. And I realized, too, come to think of it, that all this time, for thirteen years, that sepia-coloured southern snake of Midori's had been hiding what it knew. It had swallowed the secret of our being in Atami together with a flick of its red tongue, quick as a ripple of heat in the air, and then acted as if nothing had happened.

What are these snakes we carry inside us? Egotism, jealousy, destiny... the sum of all these things, I guess, a sort of karma too strong for us to fight. I regret that I will never have the occasion to learn what you meant. At any rate, these snakes inside us are pitiful creatures. I remember coming across the phrase "the sadness of living", or something close to that, in a book; as I write these words, I feel my heart brushing up against a similar emotion, irredeemably sad and cold. Oh, what is this thing we carry inside us—intolerably unpleasant, yet at the same time unbearably sad!

Having said this much, though, I realize that I still haven't shared my true self with you. When I first took up my pen to write this letter, my determination was easily blunted; I kept trying to escape, to run away from the things that scared me.

The other me, the one I didn't know about— what a nice excuse that is. I said just now that I noticed the white snake inside me for the first time today. That this was the first time it let me see it.

I was lying. That is not the truth. I have known about it, I'm sure, for ages.

*

Oh, when I recall that night, the night of 6th August, when the entire Hanshin region was transformed into an ocean of flames, I feel as though my heart could burst. Shōko and I spent the night in the air raid shelter you had designed for us, and at one point, when the B-29s returned yet again and plastered the sky overhead with their droning, I found myself suddenly plunged into a sense of pointlessness and loneliness so fierce I couldn't do anything against it. I felt so direly alone I can't even describe it. Terribly, miserably alone. After a while I couldn't bear just sitting around any longer, so I got up and stepped outside. And there you were, standing there.

The whole sky, to the west and the east, looked raw, brilliant red. The flames were moving towards your house, and yet even so you had come running to me, you were standing by the shelter's entrance. I went back into the shelter with you, and then, the second we were inside, I burst out sobbing. Both Shōko and you assumed an excess of fear had made me hysterical. I was never able to explain to you what I was feeling, not clearly—not then, not later. Forgive me. Even as I basked in the embrace of your great love, a love greater than I deserved, I was wishing I could be like you, coming to check on us in our shelter—that I could have gone and stood outside the shelter at Kadota's hospital in Hyōgo, with its clean white walls, which I had seen just once from a train window. The desire was so strong my body shook with it, and it took all my energy to hold it in, even as I choked on my tears.

And yet that wasn't the first time I noticed this sort of feeling inside me, either. To tell the truth, years earlier, in the building at the university in Kyoto, I was so taken aback when you pointed out the existence of that small, white snake inside me that I couldn't even move. Your eyes have never scared me more than they did then. I'm sure you didn't really mean anything when you spoke those words, but I felt as if you had seen straight into my heart, and it made me wince. I had been feeling ill on account of all those snakes, the real ones, but now, all at once, the queasiness vanished. I lifted my eyes slowly to your face, terrified, and as it happened—for some reason, I don't know why—you were just standing there with an unlit cigarette in your mouth, something you had never done before, gazing off at some point in the distance, a dazed look on your face. Maybe I was just imagining it, but your expression seemed emptier than any I had ever seen you wear. It lasted only a second, though; by the time you turned to look at me, you were your usual, mild self again.

Until that day, I had never managed to get a clear sense of the other me inside me, but you gave it a name, and ever since then I've thought of that second self as a little white snake. That night, I wrote about the snake in my diary. *Small white snake small white snake...* I filled up a page with those words, column after column, endlessly, all the while picturing the little snake, like a statuette, coiling around and around in perfect, taut circles, each tighter than the last, its small, pointy, drill-like head sticking straight up above the uppermost ring. Imagining the frightening, disagreeable thing I had inside me in that way—as something so clean, and in a form that seemed in some way to capture the sadness, the headlong intensity of being a woman—gave me some slight consolation. God himself, I was sure, would look upon a snake like that with tenderness and sorrow. He would pity it. Well, that was the nice story I told myself. And that night, my wickedness grew a full size larger.

Yes. I've said this much, so I might as well write it all. Please don't be angry. It has to do with that windy evening at the Atami Hotel thirteen years ago, when we vowed to be evil together, to deceive the entire world so that we could cherish our love.

That night, right after we exchanged that appalling vow, I lay down on my back on the well-starched white sheets, because I had nothing more to say, and for ages I just stared into the darkness. No other time in my life made as deep an impression on me as that period of silence. Maybe it lasted only five or six minutes. Maybe we stayed like that, not speaking, for half an hour, or an hour.

I was utterly alone then. I cradled my soul in my arms, forgetful even that you were stretched out beside me. Why, when we had just formed a united front, so to speak, to battle for our love, why, at a moment that should have been the most fulfilling, did I tumble into that helpless solitude?

That night you decided to deceive everyone, the entire world. Surely, though, you did not include me in your plan—I was the one person you would not deceive. But I had no intention of treating you as an exception. All my life, as long as I lived, I would deceive Midori, and the world—and you, and even myself… yes, that was the life I had been dealt. That realization flickered like a ghost light in the depths of my lonely soul.

I simply had to find some way to sever my fierce attachment to Kadota, a feeling that could have been either love or hatred. Because I could not forgive his infidelity, I couldn't, no matter what the nature of his transgression had been. I told myself I'd do anything, it didn't matter what became of me, as long as I could rid myself of my feelings for him. I was in agony. I was yearning, my whole body was yearning, for something that would let me smother that suffering.

And now, oh, what a travesty. Thirteen years since that night, nothing has changed.

*

To love, to be loved—how sad such human doings are. I remember once, in my second or third year at girls' school, we had a series of questions in an

English grammar exam about the active and passive forms of verbs. To hit, to be hit, to see, to be seen… and there among the other words on that list were two that sparkled brilliantly: to love, to be loved. As we were all peering down at the questions, licking our pencils, some joker, I never knew who, quietly sent a slip of paper around the room. Two options were penned there, each in a different style of handwriting: *Is it, maiden, your desire to love? Or do you rather desire to be loved?* Many circles had been drawn in ink, or in blue and red pencil, under the phrase "to be loved", but not one girl had been moved to place her mark below "to love". I was no different from the rest, of course, and I drew my own small circle underneath "to be loved". I guess even at the tender age of sixteen or seventeen, before we know much about what it means to love or be loved, our noses are still able to sniff out, instinctively, the joy of being loved.

When the girl in the seat next to mine took the paper from me, however, she glanced down at it for a moment and then, with hardly any hesitation, pencilled a big circle into the blank area beneath the words "to love". *I desire to love.* I've always remembered very clearly how I felt when I saw her do it—provoked by her intransigence, but also caught off guard, uncertain what to think. This girl was not one of the better students in our class, and she had a sort of gloomy, unremarkable air. Her hair had a reddish-brown tinge; she was always by herself. I have no way of knowing what became of her when she grew up, but now, as I write these words twenty years later, I find myself recalling, for some reason, again and again, her forlorn face.

When, at the end of her life, a woman lies quietly in bed with her face turned to the wall of death, does God allow her to feel at peace if she has tasted to the full the joy of being loved, or if she is able to declare without any trepidation that, while she may not have been very happy, she loved? I wonder, though—can any woman in this world say with real conviction, before God, that she has truly loved? No, no—I'm sure there are women like that. Maybe that thin-haired girl was among the chosen few when she grew up. A woman like that, I'm sure, would walk around with her hair in a wild tangle, her body scarred all over, her clothing ripped to shreds, and yet she would proudly lift her face and say, "Yes, I have loved." And then, having spoken those words, she would die.

Oh, it's unbearable—I wish I could escape it. But as hard as I try to chase the vision of that girl's face away, I can't do it, it keeps coming back. What is this intolerable unease that clings to me as I sit here, hours before I am to die? I suppose I am simply reaping the punishment I am due as a woman incapable of enduring the pain of loving, who wanted for herself only the joy of being loved.

*

It saddens me that after thirteen happy, enjoyable years with you I must write this letter.

I knew it would come sooner or later—this moment that never left my thoughts, when the blazing boat on the ocean finally burns itself out. I am just too exhausted to live any longer. I have the feeling that I have, at last, succeeded in giving you the truth of who I am. The fifteen or twenty minutes of life embodied in this letter are not much, but they are the truth, free from deception. They are the life I lived.

I would like to say one more thing, in closing. Our thirteen years together went by like a dream. But I was always happy, even so, because you loved me. Happier than anyone in the world.

I T HAD GROWN QUITE LATE when I finished reading these three letters to Misugi Jōsuke. I took the one he had written to me out of my desk and read it again. I kept running my eyes over and over the vaguely suggestive sentences with which he had concluded: *"My interest in hunting goes back several years, however, to a period when I was not as utterly alone as I am today, when my life, in both its public and its private dimensions, was without major disruption. Already, then, I could not do without the hunting gun on my shoulder. I mention this by way of closing."* As I kept reading those words I began, all at once, to sense in his gorgeous handwriting and its peculiar air of abandon a darkness that was almost unendurable. If I were to borrow Saiko's metaphor, I might describe it as his snake.

I stood suddenly and walked over to the north-facing window of my study, and stood there looking out into the dark March night, the trains on the government line sending out sprays of sparks in the distance. What could those three letters possibly have meant to Misugi? What knowledge could they have held out? None of the facts were new to him. He had long since come to understand the true nature of Midori's snake, and Saiko's.

I stood at the window for a long time, letting the cold wind gust against my cheeks. There was in my mental state a suggestion of drunkenness. I rested my hands on the window sill and peered out, as if Misugi's "desolate, dried-up riverbed" were visible there, into the darkness of the small garden that lay beneath my window, crowded with trees.

AFTERWORD

I began my career as a novelist in 1949, the year I published *The Hunting Gun*. My next work, *Bullfight*, earned me the Akutagawa Prize, and with that I became a true writer. When I reread these two texts now, whatever qualities and defects they may have as literature, I find myself dazzled by the beginner's enthusiasm that animated me in those days.

I was forty-two when *The Hunting Gun* and *Bullfight* were published. In the span of a man's life this is already verging on old age, but within the context of my life as a writer there is no question that this was my adolescence, and these the works of a very green novelist.

They say that, as authors mature, they follow the trajectory charted by their first writings—a rule to which, it seems, there are no exceptions. If this is correct, then *The Hunting Gun* and *Bullfight* carry within them, alongside their youthful ungainliness, something fundamental from which I have never been able to break free. For this reason, I believe I am more fully present in their pages than in any of my other texts.

Forty years have flowed by since then without my seeing them go, fifty novels of varying length, a hundred and eighty novellas... When I consider the work I have done, I feel a little like I am gazing out at a garden gone to seed. Amaryllises poking up in random places, roses whose appearance leaves much to be desired. The flowers blooming there belong to the most diverse species, large and small, transplanted from the desert and the Himalayas. Weeds are encroaching everywhere. Yes, it is an untended garden. Each time I look upon this landscape, it seems somewhat different. Sometimes, when the sun is shining, I find it filled with clarity. Other days it is sunk in shadow, hushed and gloomy. No matter how it appears to me, though, this untamed garden is me. No one else but me, all there is to me.

Just as men are born under lucky or unlucky stars, so, too, literary works are more or less blessed by fortune. Some arrive in the world perfectly formed; others are born sickly. Certain works achieve celebrity, while others languish in the shadows, condemned to huddle all their lives in an out-of-the-way corner. Whether or not a work meets with success is to some extent a matter of caprice. Works the author approves of are ignored, and vice versa. The destinies of literary works are as fickle as those of men. Among the works I have published, some have had the good fortune to be much discussed, while others were forgotten almost as soon as they saw the light of day.

An author's attachment to his works is not necessarily proportional to their success. On the contrary, he is overwhelmed by the desire to usher into the world works that he has been unable to complete, that remain unfinished. One notices this, naturally, in collections whose contents he himself has selected. This may well be their principal interest.

Some years ago, I put together a collection containing twenty-three texts: *The Hunting Gun* and *Bullfight*, which launched my career as a writer, and other novellas among the many I had written over the years with which I was particularly pleased. Had critics or readers been in charge of the selection, I have no doubt that the results would have been different.

YASUSHI INOUE
Tokyo, 1988

Originally published as the preface to the 1988 edition of
The Hunting Gun *(*Le Fusil de Chasse*)*
published by Editions Stock

THE BOOK OF PARADISE
ITZIK MANGER

THE ALLURE OF CHANEL
PAUL MORAND

SWANN IN LOVE
MARCEL PROUST

THE EVENINGS
GERARD REVE